At **THE DAVID BECKHAM ACADEMY** every day is a footballing adventure. Boys and girls come along to learn about the sport, develop their skills and have fun. But it's not just about tricks and flicks . . . As David Beckham knows, the real secret behind being a Premier League player is understanding the importance of dedication, teamwork, passion and having belief in yourself. In these pages you can meet football-mad children and follow them as they live out their dreams at The Academy.

**SO STEP INSIDE AND JOIN THE FUN!**

# Want to know what some of our readers thought of this book?

'I liked the free kick that Adam scored.
Adam was my favourite'

*Jude, age 7*

'The best thing about this story was Adam and James because Adam was kind'

*Ryan, age 7*

'I liked it when Adam and James share the Golden Boot Trophy'

*Jordan, age 10*

'My favourite character is Woody because he gives the advice'

*Jake, age 8*

'I'd give this story 10 out of 10. Adam's free kick was the best bit'

*Joe, age 9*

'I liked the free kick and when Adam and James became friends again'

*Stanley, age 6*

'I liked the twins, especially when they beat Studsy and he got sent off'

*Stephen, age 10*

EGMONT

*We bring stories to life*

First published in Great Britain 2009
by Egmont UK Limited
239 Kensington High Street, London W8 6SA



Text by Barry Hutchison
Cover and inside illustrations by Adam Relf
Cover photography by Anthony Mandler
Design by Becky Chilcott

ISBN 978 1 4052 4524 1

5 7 9 10 8 6 4

A CIP catalogue record for this title is available
from the British Library

Typeset by Avon DataSet Ltd, Bidford on Avon, Warwickshire
Printed and bound in Great Britain by the CPI Group

# THE DAVID BECKHAM ACADEMY

## TWIN TROUBLE

EGMONT

# CONTENTS

# BICKERING BROTHERS

Adam Parker stared out through the car window, watching the streets of London roll by. In the seat in front his brother, James, bounced up and down with excitement. Adam ignored him. He and James might be identical twins, but in many ways they couldn't be more different.

'Are we nearly there yet?' James asked, for what Adam thought must be the five hundredth time.

'Nearly, son, nearly,' smiled Mr Parker, not taking his eyes off the road.

'Great!' chirped James. 'I can't wait to show off my skills!'

Adam sighed. James was always showing off his footballing talent. Adam enjoyed a kick about as much as anyone, but James took things to a whole new level. All he ever wanted to do was play football and, when he wasn't playing it, he was usually talking about it. Loudly.

'Think David Beckham will be there?' asked James.

'Could be,' nodded their dad. 'You never know.'

'That would be amazing!' James gasped. Adam could see his brother's reflection in the car's wing mirror. His eyes were as wide as saucers.

Adam couldn't help but be a little excited himself. They were going to The David Beckham Academy, so there had to at least be a chance that their hero might show up.

'Even if he's not there it'll still be fun,' Adam said.

'Of course it will,' nodded Mr Parker. 'But remember, this isn't *just* about fun.'

'It's not about fun at all, Adam,' James snapped.

Adam frowned. 'Well . . . what's it about then?'

'It's about my professional future!'

'*That's* the spirit, James!' Mr Parker cheered. 'We're going to make sure you have the best possible start to your career on the field!'

'Oh,' said Adam. He thought about this for a few moments. 'What about *my* professional future?'

In the front seat, James erupted into loud snorts of laughter. Even their dad was struggling to hold back a snigger.

'*You?*' mocked James. 'You've got two left feet! You can't kick a ball to save your life! The only way you're going to have any sort of career on the field is if you become a farmer.'

'I'm not *that* bad,' said Adam, meekly.

'I scored a goal last time we played.'

'Yeah, in your own net! Who's the star player on the school team?' demanded James. 'Me, that's who! Who's got a trial for the county under-twelves? Me!'

'Who still sleeps with his teddy?' muttered Adam. 'You!'

'It's a collectable team mascot!' James shot back.

'So it's wearing a football shirt, but it's still a teddy!'

'That's enough, Adam,' said Mr Parker. 'James needs to be on top form for today.'

Adam sat back in his seat and stared out of the window. Maybe he was wrong. Maybe today wasn't going to be much fun after all. James and Dad were taking it all very seriously.

‘I’ll make you a deal, James,’ announced Mr Parker. ‘If your team wins the tournament today, I’ll buy you the new England kit. The whole thing. What do you say?’

‘Awesome!’ grinned James. ‘We’re *so* going to win!’

‘What if my team wins?’ asked Adam. ‘Do I get a kit?’

‘Yes, yes, of course,’ Dad replied hurriedly, not wanting to upset Adam.

‘I think your money will be safe,’ James smiled.

‘We *might* win!’ Adam protested.

‘You might,’ Mr Parker agreed. ‘Stranger things have happened.’

‘Only if you’re playing against a team of blindfolded monkeys,’ James laughed.

‘Now, James, leave your brother alone.

Just because he's not as good as you, that's no reason to make fun of him.' Mr Parker angled the car's rear-view mirror so he could see Adam in the back seat.

'Look, the thing is, son,' he said, softly. 'You're just not great at football. Which is fine. Really. Everyone's got their own special talent.'

'We just haven't found out what yours is yet,' James smirked.

'Maybe you should just focus on enjoying yourself and making some new friends,' continued Mr Parker. 'Don't worry too much about winning.'

'I'm not worried about winning at all,' Adam protested.

'Well . . . no, maybe not, but just don't distract James. He's got the chance to learn a lot here –'

*Here it comes*, thought Adam. *Plymouth Argyle*.

'– just like I had when I went for that trial at Plymouth Argyle.'

*Bingo!*

'So let's give him our support,' Mr Parker said. 'By all means, get stuck in and do your best, but stay out of James's way on the pitch, OK?'

'OK,' Adam nodded. He turned and looked out of the window. Dad and James were right, he wasn't any good at football.

He heard James let out a whoop of delight as the car rounded one last corner, and the enormous arches of The David Beckham Academy suddenly appeared before them.

Adam felt a twinge of excitement in his stomach. So he wasn't the best at football. So what? He enjoyed playing, and he was going to have fun at The Academy, no matter what anyone else might say!

# INTO THE ACADEMY

'Look,' said James, as he and his brother hurried up the steps of The Academy, 'I'm not saying there's anything wrong with being rubbish at football –'

'I'm *not* rubbish!' Adam argued. 'I'm . . . average.'

'Average is fine,' called Dad, who was following on behind.

'Average is *terrible*!' James cried. 'Average is worse than being rubbish. At least if you're really awful people will remember you, but no one remembers the average players . . .'

James stopped mid-sentence as he stepped through the polished glass doors and into The Academy.

'Now this,' he whistled, 'is so *not* average!'

The reception area was a hive of activity. Dozens of children and their parents chattered excitedly as they waited for the day's activities to begin. James pushed through the crowds, his eyes wide with wonder, while Adam and Mr Parker rushed to keep up.

'Check these out!' James gasped, pointing up at a long row of football shirts hanging in frames on the corridor wall. 'They've all been signed!'

'Cool,' Adam grinned. He scanned along the line of shirts, studying the signatures. 'Hey, that one's been signed by David Beckham himself!'

'Awesome!' James said. 'I wonder if he's here.'

'Maybe,' said Mr Parker, giving a shrug.

'That would just be the coolest thing ever!'

Adam nodded. Meeting David Beckham would be amazing, but he knew the day would be fantastic anyway.

As James continued staring up at the signed shirts, Adam turned his attention away. His eyes wandered to the opposite wall of the corridor, past the masses of eager children who had begun to gather in it. Pictures of David Beckham covered the walls, along with some motivational phrases.

'Teamwork,' Adam mumbled, reading one of the slogans. He liked the sound of that. James was happy to spend hours in the back garden at home, kicking the ball around on his own, but for Adam football was pointless without other people to play with. It was nice to know David Beckham thought the same way.

Suddenly, the corridor walls began to move. Adam reached out to steady himself, then realised that the walls weren't moving at all. Instead he was being jostled along by the crowd of children, who had begun filing quickly towards a set of double doors at the far end.

'Knock 'em dead, James!' cried Mr Parker, watching the twins go. 'And Adam . . . just do your best!'

Before either boy could reply, a stern-looking man with grey hair and an equally grey moustache appeared and stood with his

hands behind his back, waiting for silence.

'Now then,' he began, when it was quiet enough for him to be heard. 'Does anyone here like football?'

A dozen or more kids responded with a resounding 'Yes!'

'You'll have to forgive me, my hearing isn't what it used to be,' shrugged the man. 'I didn't catch that, so I'll ask again. Does anyone here like football?'

The roar that went up almost blew Adam's eardrums. Up in front, the man's face broke into a broad grin.

'Then you've come to the right place,' he said. 'I'm Frank Evans, Head Coach here at The David Beckham Academy. I, along with the other coaches, will be here to help you get the most out of your day with us. Shortly, you will be split up into teams, before beginning the morning training session. After that, you'll all take part in our afternoon tournament, with a trophy up for grabs for the winning team.

'What's more,' Frank continued, 'thanks to a competition being run in the local paper, today we'll be presenting a special 'Golden Boot' trophy to the top scorer.'

An excited whisper rippled through the crowd at the mention of the prize. James felt his heart skip a beat. That trophy was as good as his!

• • •

A few minutes later, Adam, James and the other boys were in the boys' changing room, getting ready for training.

Adam brushed the dirt off his old boots and began to unravel the frayed laces. On the bench next to him, James was already lacing up a brand new pair of Predator boots. The sleek black leather shone under the changing-room lights.

'Hey, where did you get those?' Adam demanded.

'Off Dad,' James shrugged.

'How come you get boots like that and I'm left with these manky old things?'

‘Because buying boots like this for me is called “an investment”. Buying them for you is called “a waste of money”.’

‘Right,’ Adam snarled, ‘that’s it! I’ve –’

He stopped as a horribly familiar voice suddenly boomed along the outside corridor.

‘Get outta my way, shrimp!’

Adam and James looked at each other

in shock. It couldn't be. He couldn't be here. Not him. Anyone but *him*!

The door to the changing room was thrown wide open, and both twins gasped in shock. An older, bigger boy stood framed in the doorway, his shaved head almost touching the top of the door frame. His beady eyes fixed on James and Adam and he let out a low, menacing cackle.

James and Adam both felt their hearts sink as Stuart Stubbs, their school's resident bully, strode into the room and began to get changed.

# TRAINING SPAIN

'Welcome to Spain,' said Woody, the man who had been introduced as the coach of Adam and James's team for the day. He smiled at them expectantly, clearly hoping for some kind of reaction. The twins and their teammates just stared blankly.

'I don't mean you're *actually* Spanish,' continued Woody. 'I mean that we'll be Team Spain for the day.' He pointed to some of the other groups who had already begun training on the pitch nearby. 'That's England, that's France, over there's Brazil, and we're Spain.'

The team all nodded in understanding.

'Good grief!' Woody cried suddenly, rubbing his eyes. 'Someone call the physio, I'm seeing double!' He smiled warmly down at the twins and looked from one to the other. 'You must be Adam and James. Or is it James and Adam?'

'He's Adam,' said James, nodding towards his brother. 'I'm James.'

'How am I going to tell you two apart?' Woody frowned.

'I'm better at football than he is,' announced James, quickly.

'And he's got brand new boots,' sighed Adam.

'So I see,' nodded Woody. 'I'll keep that in mind.' He turned to face the rest of the team. 'Right then,' he said, clapping his hands, 'we're going to start with some defence versus attack. Half of you will be on the attacking side, half in defence. These will be your positions when we get to the tournament this afternoon, so choose carefully. You've got thirty seconds to decide, starting now.'

'I'm going up front,' James told Adam. 'You'd be better staying in defence.'

'Why? I want to play up front too.'

'Don't be daft, you need skill to be a striker. In defence all you've got to do is pass the ball to a better player. There's nothing to it.'

Adam opened his mouth to argue, but it was too late. The other members of Team Spain were already taking up their positions around him, and Woody was getting ready to throw the ball in. He was stuck in defence, like it or not.

'Attackers, your job is to get the ball into the net,' Woody explained. 'Defenders, your job is to stop them. Everyone ready?' He threw the ball towards the attacking side and gave a short blow on his whistle. 'Go!'

Straight away, James lunged forwards and took the ball. He dribbled it expertly along the length of the training area, relishing the opportunity to impress.

A defender slid towards him. With a flick of his foot he brought the ball up and over the other player's outstretched leg, before swerving sideways to avoid another tackle.

'Too easy,' James laughed, steering the ball past his brother. Adam could only watch helplessly as it rocketed into the open net. Goal number one for the attacking side.

'Good work, James,' nodded Woody. 'Just remember you're not the only player out there.' He threw the ball back to the closest defender. 'Let's see some passing before we go any further. Hit that to James.'

The boy with the ball nodded, and kicked it straight towards Adam.

'I'm not James,' laughed Adam. He

knocked the ball along the ground to his brother. 'He is.'

'Sorry,' shrugged their teammate, 'you just look so alike.'

'We're identical twins,' said James. '*Identical*. The clue's kind of in the name.'

'Right, enough chit-chat,' clapped Woody. 'Let's get to work, amigos!'

• • •

The next hour passed quickly, with James hammering home another dozen goals all by himself. Even though he loved being able to show off, he was getting angry at Adam's failure to stop his attacks.

'How are we supposed to win the tournament if you can't defend properly?' he demanded. 'It's all very well me scoring goals up front, but we're going to get thrashed if you can't stop their strikers.'

'I'm doing my best!' Adam protested.

'Well, your best had better get a whole lot better, because in case you've forgotten, you're going to be up against Studsy.'

Adam followed his brother's gaze and felt his blood run as cold as ice. Over on the next training pitch, Stuart Stubbs was crashing through defenders using strength rather than skill as he headed straight for . . .

'GOAL!' roared Studsy. He turned to James and stared at him menacingly. 'Beat that!' he snarled.

'OK, amigos, time for the next drill,' Woody announced. 'Good effort, Adam.'

Adam smiled weakly and sloped off. *Good effort*, he thought, *but not good enough*. As he walked, he idly swung his foot and connected hard with a stray ball. It gave

a *whoosh* as it sailed through the air, and flew straight into the back of a distant net.

Woody let out a low whistle and rubbed his chin thoughtfully. 'Now that,' he said to himself, 'was quite a free kick.'

# LUNCHTIME ENCOUNTER

Adam and James were breathing heavily as they and the other children filed off the pitch in the direction of the canteen. Woody and the other coaches had worked them all hard, and they'd built up a real appetite.

'I don't know what they're cooking, but it smells great,' puffed Adam, as the aroma from the canteen reached his nose.

'I don't *care* what it is,' James grinned, 'I'm so hungry I'd eat anything!'

'Anything?'

‘Anything,’ James nodded.

‘What about . . . slugs on toast?’

‘Two bites and they’d be gone.’

‘Yuck! You’re disgusting,’ laughed Adam.

‘What?’ asked James, fighting back laughter of his own. ‘I love the taste of slugs on toast!’

‘I hope you like the taste of defeat too,’ growled a voice in James’s ear.

‘I wouldn’t know,’ James sniffed. ‘I’ve never tried it. What’s it like?’

‘You think you’re smart, don’t you?’ Studsy hissed. ‘But I’m warning you, try to be smart out on the pitch this afternoon and you’ll regret it.’

‘Oh, yeah?’ James scowled, stepping closer to Studsy and staring up at him. ‘I’m not scared of you!’

Adam winced. Telling Stuart Stubbs you weren't scared of him wasn't a sensible thing to do. It would normally lead to him doing something extremely painful to you – often in slow motion. After that, even the bravest souls tended to get scared and stay that way.

'Really?' Studsy sneered. 'Well, I'll have to see what I can do about that.'

Moving surprisingly quickly for someone his size, he lunged and pushed James hard on the chest, sending him staggering backwards.

'What's going on here?' demanded Woody, dashing over from one of the nearby tables. 'Were you two fighting?'

'He started it!' cried Studsy.

'What!' James spluttered. 'I did not!'

'I don't care who started it,' Woody told them. 'I'm very surprised at you, Adam.'

'I'm James.'

'I'm very surprised at you, James,' the coach continued quickly. 'Now will someone tell me what this was about?'

'The Golden Boot Trophy,' James shrugged. 'He wants to ruin my chances of winning it.'

'Yeah, like you even had a chance,' Studsy muttered.

'Neither of you will have a chance if you carry on like that,' Woody said. 'Being a top striker needs a level head under pressure. That means controlling your temper.' He stared at the boys for a few moments, letting his words sink in. 'Now,' he said at last, 'go and get your lunch.'

• • •

James idly swirled his spaghetti round on his plate, ignoring the stares and silent threats from Studsy, who was sitting two tables away.

'I thought you were starving,' smiled Adam, sliding on to the bench next to his brother.

'Not any more,' James mumbled.

'Don't let Studsy get to you,' urged

Adam. 'You're a much better player than he is. You'll definitely win the Golden Boot.'

'Look, just stop, OK?' James snapped. 'I don't care what you think.'

Adam frowned. James could be moody sometimes, but this was worse than he'd ever seen him. 'I was only trying to help,' he said.

'*Help?*' scoffed James. 'What, like you *helped* me when Studsy attacked me? What if Woody hadn't jumped in? What would you have done?'

'I'd have done my best!'

'Oh, yeah, like you always do. Good old Adam, always doing his best. Well, guess what? Your best is terrible.'

'Hey, wait, what did I do?' Adam asked, shocked by his brother's outburst.

'That's exactly it, you did *nothing*! He

was threatening me and you did *nothing*!' James dropped his fork into his uneaten pasta. 'I used to think you were just a useless footballer,' he said, 'but I was wrong. You're a useless brother too.'

Lost for words, Adam could only watch as James got up from the table and stomped off in the direction of the boys' changing room. What James had said was out of order, but what if he was right? What if he really *was* useless? The team had worked hard all morning to prepare for the tournament, but if what James said was true, then he would almost certainly let them down!

# LEVEL PEGGING

'Great game, my Spanish amigos!' said Woody, applauding the team as they filed off the pitch. 'Well done, James, but don't forget you're allowed to pass to the others too. I'm sure they might even enjoy getting to kick the ball for a bit.'

James nodded at the coach, but otherwise didn't respond. What was the point in passing? None of the team could knock home goals like he could.

'Hey, that was some hat-trick!' beamed Adam, giving his brother a congratulatory slap on the back. 'You were on fire out there!'

'At least one of us was,' James scowled. 'I can't believe you let their strikers get past you so easily. That goal they got was your fault.'

'Come on,' pleaded Adam, 'it was just a mistake. We still won.'

'No thanks to you,' James snorted, before marching off to get a drink.

'Fantastic goals, James,' cheered one of the twins' teammates as he strolled past. He gave Adam a playful punch on the arm.

'James is the other one,' sighed Adam.

'Oh. Sorry.' The boy thought for a moment. 'Still, good defending though!'

'Thanks,' Adam mumbled.

Over on the touchline, James gulped down some water and wiped the sweat from his forehead. He'd been running around like crazy all afternoon, and the most important game of the whole tournament would be starting in just a few minutes.

'Great work out there, son!' cried Mr Parker, running over to James. 'The other parents and I were allowed in just before the final whistle. That last-minute goal was *incredible*!'

'Thanks,' replied James. 'We've won all our games, so we've got maximum points.'

'Brilliant!' his dad exclaimed. 'So does that mean you win the trophy?'

'Not yet. Holland have won all their games too, so we're level pegging. We play them next.'

Mr Parker nodded and looked in the direction of the other team who were limbering up nearby.

'Hey, doesn't that boy go to your school?' he asked. 'Steven, isn't it?'

'Stuart,' said James flatly. 'And, yes, he does.'

'Aw, that must've been nice for you, having a school friend here to play with.'

Studsy caught James looking at him and glared back.

'Yeah,' said James unconvincingly.

'We've both scored six goals in the tournament so far, so I need to knock a few more in if I'm going to win the Golden Boot.'

'Hi, Dad!' chirped Adam, joining his family.

'Hi, Adam. Having fun?'

'I am, actually!' Adam began. 'It's really been a –'

'Great stuff,' Mr Parker nodded, before turning his attention back to James. 'So you're going to win this last game, right?'

'Should do.'

'No "should do" about it,' scolded Mr Parker. 'You're going to win this last game. Say it.'

'We're going to win this last game,' repeated James.

'Say it like you mean it! We're going to win this last game!'

'We're going to win this last game,' repeated James, louder this time.

'I am a footballing machine,' said his dad.

'Er . . . I am a footballing machine.'

'I will defeat anyone who gets in my way!' cried Mr Parker, getting a bit carried away.

'Um . . . Dad,' James winced. You're being a bit weird.'

'What?' frowned Mr Parker. He glanced round and realised the other parents were giving him funny looks. 'I . . . uh . . . yes. Just, you know, do what you can.' He gave an embarrassed cough. 'That's all I ask.'

'Spain versus Holland,' announced one

of the coaches out on the pitch. 'Teams in position, please.'

'Good luck!' yelled Mr Parker, as he watched his sons head back out on to the pitch. Woody ran after them, trying to get their attention.

'Adam, could I have a quick word?' he asked, catching the closest twin by the arm.

'I'm James. The boots, remember?'

Woody looked down and spotted James's shiny black Predator boots. 'Right, so you are,' he nodded, releasing his grip. As James headed for the centre circle, Woody caught up with the real Adam.

'Hey, Adam,' he smiled, 'I've noticed you've been taking some criticism today.'

'Yeah,' shrugged Adam. 'It's fine.'

'Well, do you know what I say? Ignore it. I've been watching your progress and

you're a great team player. Really. Some people forget that football's a team game. You understand that though, and you make the team stronger for it.'

'Um . . . thanks,' mumbled Adam. He wasn't used to receiving compliments and wasn't quite sure how to react.

'And you've got a really powerful right foot on you too,' Woody continued.

'Get that foot behind a free kick and no one is going to stop that ball! All you need is to believe that you can do it, OK? Be confident in yourself and stay focused.'

'OK!' Adam nodded. He couldn't hide the wide grin that had spread across his face. That was quite probably the nicest thing anyone had ever said to him.

'Good lad,' Woody replied. He laid a hand on Adam's shoulder and gave it a friendly squeeze. 'Now, amigo, it's time to go out there and show everyone *exactly* what you can do!'

# THE BIG MATCH

James waited by the centre spot, the ball at his feet. Just beyond the circle, Studsy was impatiently pacing back and forth. Up above, a downpour of rain began to rattle against the domed roof of The Academy. James ignored it. There was only one sound he was listening for.

*Peeeeeeeeeeeeep!* The whistle blew, and the game kicked off. After a quick 'one-two' manoeuvre, James took the ball and charged up the pitch. Studsy slid in with a late tackle, but James flicked the ball up and over him, making the bully roar with rage.

As the goalmouth came into view, James spun left, easily avoiding the clumsy tackle of the first defender. He weaved right, dodging another with no trouble. He slammed his foot into the ball, sending it rocketing towards the goalmouth. The goalkeeper threw himself sideways, arms outstretched in desperation, but there was no way he could reach it.

'GOAL!' screamed Mr Parker. Overhead, the rain battering on the roof sounded almost like wild applause.

James returned to his own half, and Holland kicked off. Two midfielders passed the ball around patiently, before passing it through to Studsy. The bully immediately began thundering downfield.

The first defender was knocked out of

his way easily, closely followed by a second. In the blink of an eye, Studsy had broken down the defence, leaving only Adam to beat.

'Don't let him past!' cried James. 'Tackle him!'

Teeth gritted, Adam flew at the ball. He couldn't let the team down. Unseen by the referee, Studsy thrust out an elbow, and Adam felt a sharp pain explode in his ribcage. Before he could catch his breath, Studsy was past him. Adam groaned as the bully struck home the equaliser.

'You idiot!' James shouted as Adam struggled to his feet. He returned to the centre, still muttering about his twin's terrible tackling. Two of his teammates took the kick-off, but Studsy was ready for them. He ploughed straight through, controlled the ball, and was halfway to the goalmouth before anyone could react.

'Not again,' gasped Adam. He tried desperately to stop the charge, but in the end could only watch as Studsy slammed another goal into the back of the net, sending his team into a 2–1 lead.

'You *double* idiot!' James cried, seeing his chances of winning the Golden Boot slipping away.

'Silly mistakes,' sighed Mr Parker.

Adam stood in the middle of the pitch, staring down at his tatty boots in shame. They were right, he *was* useless, and now everyone could see it.

'Don't give up, Adam,' called another voice. Adam glanced up and spotted Woody watching on. 'You can do this, I know you can.'

Adam nodded. If Woody believed in him, maybe it was time he started believing in himself.

Studsy was on a roll. As soon as Spain kicked off, he took the ball, shouldering midfielders out of the way as he mounted yet another attack.

'Not so rough, Stuart,' Woody warned.

Adam took a deep breath. Studsy was past one defender now, and closing fast. *You can do this*, he told himself. *You can do it*.

As the striker drew near, Adam darted forward, his eye fixed on the ball. He only had one chance.

He slid to the ground, ducking under Studsy's sharp elbows. His toe poked the ball away from the bully and into the clear in a perfect tackle.

'*Yes!*' cheered Woody.

HOME
AWAY

Lunging past Studsy, Adam punted the ball the length of the pitch.

James blinked in amazement, before realising the ball was curving straight towards him! Throwing himself backwards, he swung a leg up in an overhead kick. His boot connected hard with the ball, just before he hit the ground.

Flat on his back, James watched the net shake and heard the crowd roar. He had put them level again!

As James celebrated with the rest of the team, Adam glanced up at the clock. Two minutes to go. They could still win this! They could still win the trophy!

Holland kicked off and began to move quickly up the pitch. More confident now, Adam sprinted forwards and intercepted a pass.

'Great move!' shouted Mr Parker. 'Now give it to James!'

Adam looked up, found his brother and lobbed the ball to him. James brought the high ball down and spun, readying for a last-minute shot on goal.

*CRUNCH!*

James cried out in agony and slumped to the ground, as Studsy brought a boot down hard on his ankle.

*Peeeeeeeeeeeeeep!*

'Right, Stuart, that's it,' said Woody, flashing a red card in Studsy's direction. 'You're off the park.' The bully just shrugged.

'Animal!' cried Mr Parker. 'Learn to control yourself!'

'That's my son,' growled a menacing voice. Mr Parker turned and found himself staring at the largest man he had ever seen. Studsy's dad looked even meaner than his son.

'Oh . . .' whimpered Mr Parker. 'Congratulations.'

Over on the pitch, Woody helped James to his feet. 'Can you go on?'

'I'm fine. I – AAAAH!' James yelped as he put his weight on his ankle. It was no use, he was out of the game.

With just a few seconds left of the match and the scores level, the coaches signalled for Spain to take a free kick.

The remaining players glanced at each other nervously. This would be the final kick of the game and their chance to claim the trophy, but with their star player out of action, who could possibly fill his boots?

# THE SWITCH

'Come on now, lads, you need to decide which one of you is taking the free kick,' said Woody, pointing to his watch. 'We haven't got all day.'

'Well, there's no way *I'm* doing it,' announced one boy, folding his arms. 'What if I miss? I'll look like a total idiot!'

'But if you score you'll be a hero!' said another. 'Everyone will be cheering your name. Wouldn't that be brilliant?'

'You do it then!'

'No *way*, I might miss!'

Adam sighed and looked across at James, who was sitting on a bench by the sidelines, rubbing his ankle and looking miserable. For all his boasting and bragging, James was by far the best player on the team. If he hadn't been playing for them, there was no way Spain would have made it anywhere near this far. He deserved to be the one to take the free kick, but Studsy had stolen that chance from him.

*Unless*, thought Adam, as an idea suddenly struck him.

Leaving the others to bicker amongst themselves, he strolled over and began to talk quietly to his brother.

'Your boots,' he hissed. 'Give them to me.'

'What?' spluttered James. 'No way, these

are *mine*! Just because you got a couple of half-decent passes in doesn't mean you can just *have* them!'

'Look, there's no time to explain, just shut up and give me the boots or I'll kick your sore ankle.'

'You wouldn't dare!'

'Try me.'

Adam sighed. 'OK, take them! Here.'

James tugged at the laces of the shiny Predator boots and pulled them off. Glancing around to make sure no one was looking, Adam kicked off his own tatty boots and pulled the new pair on. He leaped to his feet and immediately felt like he was walking on air.

'Wow, these are *amazing*!' he gasped, bouncing up and down on the spot, 'I've got to get a pair of these!' He threw his own boots across to James. 'Stick these on, quick.'

'Ewww,' James shuddered. 'I can't believe you're making me to put these manky old things on.'

'Everything OK there, lads?' asked Woody, who was making his way over to the twins. 'How are you feeling now, James?'

'You know, my ankle's a lot better, actually,' said Adam, before his brother had a chance to reply. 'I think I can go back on and take that free kick after all.'

'What?' James frowned. 'But you're –'

'No, really, *Adam*,' said Adam, firmly. 'I'll be fine. You do want me to win the Golden Boot, don't you?'

James hesitated for a moment, before realising at last what Adam's plan was.

'Um . . . yes,' he nodded quickly. 'I do. I really do.' He gave his brother a warm smile. 'Good luck.'

'Thanks. I'll need it,' replied Adam, returning the smile. He turned and jogged back on to the pitch, limping slightly to make things look more realistic. Up ahead, he heard his team give a loud cheer of relief. Behind him, Studsy groaned loudly. Adam's plan was working. Everyone thought he was James. Everyone that is, except their dad.

'What's going on?' demanded Mr Parker, appearing at James's side. 'What's he playing at? This is a crucial kick! Adam can't do it, can he?'

'D'you know what, Dad?' grinned James. 'I think maybe he can!'

Just outside the Holland box, Adam picked up the ball. He threw it up in the air a few times and caught it, pretending to test the weight. In reality, he was trying to get his nerves under control. Was he really going to do this? Was he really going to take the kick that would decide the outcome of the entire tournament? Had he gone stark raving bonkers?

'You can do it, James!' cried one of the team.

'Knock it in for us!' yelled another.

Adam felt his heart begin to thud faster and faster against the inside of his chest, as he rested the ball on the spot indicated by the referee and took a few paces back.

He eyed up the net. The wall of Holland players had most of the goalmouth covered, and the keeper seemed to be guarding the small area that was left. There was a tiny gap though – barely even bigger than the ball – which looked to be unprotected. If he could curve the ball into that space then his team would win the tournament, and James would win the Golden Boot. The chances of him being able to hit so small a target were almost non-existent though. He felt his hopes sink. It was too difficult. There was no way he could score.

'I believe in you, son,' called a voice from the sidelines. Adam turned and saw his dad watching proudly on. From the look on his face, Adam knew Mr Parker had figured out the plan. Adam felt a lump forming in his throat. Dad was saying he believed in *him*, for once!

That did it! He was going to make his dad proud. He was going to make James proud. Most importantly of all, he was going to make *himself* proud.

Taking a final, steadying breath, Adam focused his gaze on the gap in Holland's defence, and began his run-up!

# THE FINAL WHISTLE

For a few long moments, the whole world seemed to hold its breath. As his foot struck the ball, Adam tilted his body backwards, curving the shot towards the goal. Every eye in the arena followed its path through the air.

The largest member of the Holland wall leaped upwards, hoping to put himself between the ball and the net. He felt a wind whip past his head. The boy was tall, but he wasn't quite tall enough.

The keeper dived to where he thought

the ball was flying, arms at full stretch. An excited gasp went round The Academy. Adam craned his neck, trying to follow the path of the ball as it dipped behind the wall of Holland players. He bit his lip. Had it gone in?

'GOAL!' cried Mr Parker. Adam threw up his hands in excitement and turned to see his dad charging on to the pitch, beaming proudly. He yelped with delight as Dad scooped him up and spun him round in a wide circle, hugging him tightly. 'You did it!' Mr Parker exclaimed. 'You did it!'

The other members of Team Spain rushed over, cheering wildly. 'You did it, James! You won the Golden Boot!'

'James?' Mr Parker frowned. 'No, but he's –'

'I did!' said Adam, glancing meaningfully at his dad. 'Just lucky, I guess!'

'Ladies and gentleman,' beamed Frank, who had come to join the celebrations. 'The winner of the Golden Boot Trophy – James Parker!' Another round of loud cheering echoed through The Academy.

'I said today was a special day because of the top-scorer trophy,' the head coach continued, 'but that's not the only reason it's special.' The players and parents began whispering to each other. What did he mean?

With a creak, the doors leading to the tunnel slowly opened. Everyone turned to look as a familiar figure stepped through. Adam's mouth dropped almost all the way to the floor.

'Here to present the trophies today,'

Woody beamed, 'I give you Mr David Beckham!'

A deafening roar rose up, as everyone around the pitch area jumped to their feet. Unnoticed, Adam darted across to his brother and began to kick off his boots.

'Quick,' he hissed, 'change back so you can get your trophy!'

James didn't need telling twice. He pulled open the laces of Adam's old boots and slipped his feet out. He couldn't believe it! He was about to be presented with the top-scorer trophy by David Beckham himself!

He looked up at his brother, remembering a word he'd seen written on the wall earlier: *Teamwork*. At the time he'd thought it was stupid, but suddenly he wasn't so sure.

'I . . . um . . . I haven't been very nice to you,' James said, slipping his own boots back on.

'What?' muttered Adam. 'Oh. Doesn't matter. Forget it.'

'No, but I –'

'Look, hurry up!' Adam replied, flashing his brother a broad smile. 'Unless you don't want to meet David Beckham, of course!'

'You ready to collect your trophy, James?' grinned Woody, hurrying over.

James looked at his brother, who nodded at him. 'Well, coach,' James began, 'the thing is . . .'

Woody listened as James filled him in on everything that had happened.

'So you see, it wasn't me who scored that final goal, it was Adam,' concluded

James. 'So if anyone deserves the Golden Boot, it's him.'

Woody glanced between the twins. They swallowed hard, unsure how the coach would take the news.

'Well, then,' he said finally. 'In that case, I suggest you *both* go collect the trophy!'

'Those were some really impressive performances out there, lads.'

'T-thanks,' stammered Adam.

'You're David Beckham,' croaked James, his throat dry.

'And that was a fantastic free kick at the end,' smiled David. 'I couldn't have done better myself!'

'Wow! Thank you!' Adam beamed.

James swallowed hard. 'Y-You're David Beckham!'

'Yes, I am,' David laughed. He held up the trophy – a shiny gold-coloured football boot mounted on a plinth. 'Congratulations, it seems you *both* deserve this.'

The twins took the trophy and held it up above their heads as the crowd went wild. They turned to show their dad, but he was nowhere to be seen.

'We did it,' said Adam proudly.

'That's David Beckham!' was all James could say in reply.

'Yes,' chuckled his brother. 'It definitely is!'

• • •

Half an hour later, Mr Parker unlocked the car and his sons jumped in. Adam cried out in shock as he sat on something uncomfortable.

'Hey!' he gasped. 'A new pair of Predator boots!'

'They're all yours, son,' his dad said. 'I realised I wasn't exactly supportive of you earlier, so I nipped out and collected them when you were getting the trophy.' He smiled. 'Make sure you have fun with them.'

'Oh, I will! Thanks, Dad!'

'You do realise this causes a big

problem, don't you?' grinned James, giving his brother a sly wink.

'Oh?' frowned Mr Parker. 'Why's that?'

Adam laughed as he tried the boots on for size. They were a perfect fit. 'Now no one will be able to tell us apart!'

TURN THE PAGE TO READ A SNEAK PREVIEW OF

# LE FOOTBALL

THE SECOND BOOK IN THE DAVID BECKHAM ACADEMY SERIES!

# NEW ARRIVALS

Luke Chapman was having the best game of his whole life. He'd just scored two brilliant goals for his team and no one was going to stop him making it a hat-trick.

'Go on, Luke, you can do it!' yelled his lanky friend Max, who was playing in goal on Luke's side.

'This is my chance!' Luke muttered as a striker on the other team dribbled the ball towards him. With amazing speed, Luke flew at it, sliding in for a perfect tackle. The ball sprang free and Luke was up and after it in a flash. He got it under control with ease, dodged past a defender, then went charging towards the goal.

'Go on!' cried Oliver, another friend, as Luke's foot connected hard with the ball. It slammed straight into the back of the net.

'Yesss!' roared Luke, as the whistle blew for full time.

'We did it!' cheered Max. He started singing a victory chant: 'Three–nil, three–nil, three–nil, *three–nil*!'

Luke was grinning as the three boys headed back to the changing rooms. It was only his second day at The David Beckham Academy, but in that time he'd made two new mates and was playing better football than ever before.

'You were awesome,' said Oliver, slapping Luke on the back.

'Cheers,' said Luke. 'Guess I had some luck in that game.'

'*Luck?*' repeated Oliver. 'More like pure skill, I reckon. I wish I was half as good as you!'

'You're pretty good yourself, Olly,' smiled Luke.

'Well, maybe, but I bet you're the one who'll be a professional in a few years.'

'Yeah, well . . .' he shrugged.

Embarrassed, Luke ran his hand through his short brown hair. He was used to being the best player on the pitch, but he didn't like to go round boasting about it.

'Anyway, you made some world-class tackles just now,' said Luke. 'And you're brilliant at tactics.'

'Oh, tactics is just classroom stuff,' said Oliver, pulling a face. 'It's what you do on the pitch that counts.'

'Having short fat legs doesn't help much, does it?' said Max behind them, playfully trying to trip Oliver up.

'Hey, stop it,' snapped Oliver. 'I didn't notice you doing much just now!'

'What do you mean?' said Max, surprised.

'Well, every time a striker came anywhere near you, Luke rushed him and got the ball away!'

'Maybe he did,' frowned Max. 'But it takes real skill to be a goalie, y'know!'

'What, you mean standing up straight and trying not to fall asleep?' Oliver teased.

'No, *I don't* mean that,' replied Max.

'Oh, you mean being tall and lanky?'

giggled Oliver. 'Cos that's not skill either.'

'Oi, you! I made some good saves in that game!' Max protested.

Luke laughed at his two friends. They just couldn't resist winding each other up!

Later on in the changing room, the boys had just finished getting dressed when they suddenly heard a loud voice booming across the room.

'OK, everyone, could I have your attention, please? I've got a very important announcement to make!'

The voice belonged to Frank Evans, head coach of The Academy. He had grey hair, a big grey moustache and right now his eyebrows were knitted together crossly. Everyone stopped talking and listened.

'Wonder what it is?' whispered Oliver. 'Is David Beckham coming or something?'

'*Ssshhh!*' hissed Max.

Mr Evans looked sternly at Max and Oliver, then cleared his throat importantly.

'Now, as you all know, the next World Cup is just a few months away, and to celebrate we've been taking part in a special football exchange scheme. For the rest of the week a boys' team from France will be joining you. This only happens once in a while, so I hope you'll all give them a very warm welcome.'

Just then, Max put his hand up and started waving it about.

'Yes, Max, what is it?' said Frank.

'Do you want us to thrash them?'

Everyone sniggered and Frank cleared his throat again.

'I expect you to do your very best, of course,' he said. 'But the most important thing is that you show them everything that's good about English football. I want to see teamwork, dedication and good, all-round sportsmanship.'

Whispers of excitement echoed around the room and Oliver turned to Luke, grinning. 'Let's show them what's good about English footy,' he said. 'You'll blow them away!'

One by one, the French team filed into the changing room, looking slightly nervous.

'Right,' continued Frank. 'I'd like you all to line up and give our guests a welcoming handshake.'

As the two lines of boys shuffled past each other, they all smiled and shook hands.

'Hi, I'm Luke,' said Luke as he came to the last boy in the line.

'Louis,' replied the boy. He was taller than Luke, with long dark hair. He looked very strong.

'It's really good here,' said Luke. 'You're going to have a brilliant time.' He held out his hand and Louis shook it in silence, then turned away sharply and walked off with his teammates.

Luke was left slightly puzzled. 'Hmmm,' he murmured to himself. 'Was it something I said?'

# Collect all the books in The David Beckham Academy range

## STORYBOOKS

| | | |
|---|---|---|
| Twin Trouble | ISBN 978 1 4052 4524 1 | £4.99 |
| Le Football | ISBN 978 1 4052 4525 8 | £4.99 |
| Save the Day | ISBN 978 1 4052 4526 5 | £4.99 |
| Bossy Boots | ISBN 978 1 4052 4527 2 | £4.99 |

## ACTIVITY BOOKS

| | | |
|---|---|---|
| How-to Handbook | ISBN 978 1 4052 4669 9 | £4.99 |
| Ultimate Football Sticker Book | ISBN 978 1 4052 4670 5 | £4.99 |

## ANNUAL

| | | |
|---|---|---|
| 2010 Annual | ISBN 978 1 4052 4644 6 | £7.99 |

## EGMONT PRESS: ETHICAL PUBLISHING

Egmont Press is about turning writers into successful authors and children into passionate readers – producing books that enrich and entertain. As a responsible children's publisher, we go even further, considering the world in which our consumers are growing up.

**Safety First**
Naturally, all of our books meet legal safety requirements. But we go further than this; every book with play value is tested to the highest standards – if it fails, it's back to the drawing-board.

**Made Fairly**
We are working to ensure that the workers involved in our supply chain – the people that make our books – are treated with fairness and respect.

**Responsible Forestry**
We are committed to ensuring all our papers come from environmentally and socially responsible forest sources.

**For more information, please visit our website at www.egmont.co.uk/ethical**

Egmont is passionate about helping to preserve the world's remaining ancient forests. We only use paper from legal and sustainable forest sources, so we know where every single tree comes from that goes into every paper that makes up every book.

This book is made from paper certified by the Forestry Stewardship Council (FSC), an organisation dedicated to promoting responsible management of forest resources. For more information on the FSC, please visit **www.fsc.org**. To learn more about Egmont's sustainable paper policy, please visit **www.egmont.co.uk/ethical**.